About the Author

Kevin Ponciroli, M.D. has been taking care of kids for over 16 years. As a pediatrician, he has helped many parents navigate the challenges of raising children and stresses the importance of books and reading at every stage of development.

As a husband and father, he has helped raise three wonderful girls, and during that time he has worn many entertainer hats: singer, dancer, comedian, and story-teller. And while "potty-trainer" may not be the most glorious of fatherly duties, it did help inspire the writing of this book. And for the record, his Ünderpanties of choice are boxers with balloon animals on them.

Velcome to Ünderpanties

(oon-der-pan-teez)

Kevin Ponciroli

Velcome to Ünderpanties
(oon-der-pan-teez)

Olympia Publishers
London

www.olympiapublishers.com
OLYMPIA PAPERBACK EDITION

A CIP catalogue record for this title is available from the British Library.

ISBN: 978-1-78830-601-0

First Published in 2020

Olympia Publishers
Tallis House
2 Tallis Street
London
EC4Y 0AB

Printed in Great Britain

Dedication

For Isabella, Olivia, and Amelia. Thank you for demanding the same bed-time story every night and encouraging me to share it with the world.

Millie was so excited.
Tomorrow was a really big day.
She had stayed dry for an entire month.
She shouted, "Hip, hip, hooray!

I haven't had an accident,
for such a very long time.
I'm ready for my big girl underpants.
A pair that is all mine."

With so many options available,
they discussed which kind she would prefer.
Her mom and dad gave her a great big hug.
They were so proud of her.

As Millie closed her eyes in her bed,
she wondered what kind they would be.
Flowers? Polka-dots? Princesses? Ponies?
She could not wait to see.

"Wake up sleepy-head. We're here."
Millie slowly opened her eyes.
Her dad was carrying her off an airplane,
but that was just the start of her surprise.

She looked around a bit confused,
but her silence was very brief.
"You can see everyone's underpants!"
Millie yelled in disbelief.

All the workers were running around,
doing their jobs at the airport.
But over top of their clothes, in plain view,
were undergarments of every sort.

A man was standing in front of the plane
wearing a suit, which looked normal at first glance.
Except he had a pair of striped boxer shorts
worn on top of his dress pants.

"I am Mayor Debrief,
und on behalf of our fair town,
vee invite all friends and fizitors
to schtay awhile, und get a good look around.

For here, vee celebrate our favorite type of clothink
und honor it vith zongs und chanties.
Vee don't dare hide zem BENEAZ our clothes.
Velcome to Ünderpanties.

Please fizit our many fine buzinesses,
especially zee tailor vere Ünderpanties are sewn.
Und don't forget zee town's gift schop,
vere you can buy a pair of your fery own."

As her parents finished thanking everyone
for their much-appreciated hospitality,
Millie noticed peoples' underwear
showed a lot of their own personality.

Pilots were walking about
wearing some that had tiny airplanes.
Gardeners' had flowers. Drivers' had cars.
Doctors' had bones, muscles, and brains.

Millie's parents smiled at her and said,
"Let's go find a pair you can use."
Millie got excited and a little nervous.
How would she ever be able to choose?

They all left the airport,
and went to go explore.
Main Street was lined with quaint little shops.
Their first stop was a bookstore.

Customers filled the aisles
looking at books from their favorite genres.
There were infants, teenagers, grandparents,
and even soon-to-be new mommas.

"Vat can I help you find?"
asked the lady who owned the shop.
With so many different sections of books,
the variety of Ünderpanties was non-stop.

Everyone was wearing
their favorite story-book characters:
wizards, farmers, aliens, animals –
even some with writers or editors.

Not seeing anything she liked,
Millie hurriedly ran outside.
This place was overwhelming
and really wasn't helping her to decide.

So the family continued
on their Ünderpanties walking tour.
Next stop, the local diner - "Best Place to Eat" –
according to the official town brochure.

The servers, waitresses, and busboys
all displayed love for their favorite food,
but the family got a little worried
after seeing the chef's were partly barbecued.

Everyone sat down and ordered
and had a mighty fine meal.
They left to continue their Ünderpanty search.
Who knew this would be such an ordeal?

As they walked out, Millie spotted Knicker Park
and begged her parents to go on the swings.
The park was full of families
doing a ton of other fun things.

Kids were flying kites
and tossing the frisbee around.
She watched the soccer and baseball teams
and the kids on the merry-go-round.

All of a sudden, Millie's eyes lit up,
she took a breath and said, "Mom, I beg your pardon.
Do you think we could go over there
and check out the really neat garden?"

The variety of flowers was astounding.
The aroma was simply magical.
Flowers had always been Millie's most favorite thing.
Even her room looked downright botanical.

"Millie dear, it's getting late," said Mom.
"We've had a great time, but now we have to leave.
There's one more place we have to visit.
And one very important item we need."

In the middle of the town square
was the biggest store Millie had ever seen.
It was the Ünderpanties main gift shop.
But what item did her mom mean?

"Potty training is done, big girl.
No more diapers for you to wear.
There sure is a lot to choose from.
Now go and find your favorite pair."

Millie frantically ran around the aisles,
the number of choices boggling her mind.
But there, shining in the window,
she saw the most perfect kind.

Excitedly, she bolted across the store
weaving in and out of the townsfolk.
But just as she was about to grab them . . .

Poof, from her bed, she suddenly awoke.

Lying in bed she realized,
the entire adventure was a dream.
Ünderpanties was such a great place.
But it wasn't real, or so it would seem.

Feeling a little disappointed and sad,
Millie opened the door and walked out.
Mom and Dad were there holding a present.
She giggled and began to shout.

"What is that? Is it for me?
Is it what I've been trying so hard to get?"
She grabbed the present from Mom's hand
and flew to her room like a jet.

She ripped open the package to find
the present she worked so hard to earn –
a bright pink pair of bikini bottoms
with a purplely daisy pattern.

It was the same pair she had dreamed about.
She could not have been more glad.
She immediately put them on
and gave a hug to her mom and dad.

"I love my Ünderpanties so very much!"
Millie said with a smile as bright as a gem.
Her parents looked at her a little confused.
"Uh, honey. What did you just call them?"

CPSIA information can be obtained
at www.ICGtesting.com
Printed in the USA
LVHW060756171120
671902LV00010B/255

9 781788 306010